William Ferguson

Rhymes on Various Subjects

William Ferguson

Rhymes on Various Subjects

ISBN/EAN: 9783337264383

Printed in Europe, USA, Canada, Australia, Japan

Cover: Foto ©Andreas Hilbeck / pixelio.de

More available books at **www.hansebooks.com**

ON

VARIOUS SUBJECTS.

BY

WILLIAM FERGUSON,

R. W. FUSILIERS.

CALCUTTA:

PRINTED BY THACKER, SPINK AND CO.

1883.

TO

THE OFFICERS,

NON-COMMISSIONED OFFICERS AND MEN

OF THE

1ST BATTALION, ROYAL WELSH FUSILIERS,

THIS LITTLE VOLUME

IS RESPECTFULLY DEDICATED

BY

THEIR HUMBLE SERVANT,

THE AUTHOR.

PREFACE.

THE effusions contained in this small work have nearly all appeared in various public journals at different times, and are now collected and published in book form, because the writer has been led to believe that many men of the Regiment he is attached to would like such a volume as a sort of Regimental *souvenir*.

This then, and not any favourable opinion as to the merits of the various pieces, is the reason for their publication; and it is to be hoped that a knowledge of this fact may disarm hostile criticism.

The writer is conscious that his perform-
ances are very humble, but such as they are,
his subscribers are welcome to them, and he
sincerely trusts this little book may be pre-
served by many who will look back with
pleasure to the time spent in the Royal
Welsh Fusiliers.

WM. FERGUSON,

School Master,

R. W. Fusiliers.

DUM-DUM,

1st July 1883.

CONTENTS.

RHYMES ON VARIOUS SUBJECTS.

The Defence of Rorke's Drift.

Shade of that bard who, on the Ægean strand,
  In stateliest numbers, sang of Troy divine,
Grant that one spark from out the sacred flame,
  Which fired thy soul, may now enlighten mine,
To sing of those thy Muse might well have sung—
  Men unsurpassed by him of Priam's line,
Or by his conqueror, Thetis' god-like son,
  Or all those kings and chiefs who crossed the
    brine
To war with Troy for Argive Helen's sake,
And force her back to bonds she fain would break !

The world has changed since Ilium's doom was
    sealed,
    And war has changed too, with the changing
    years ;
But hearts still glow when heroes' deeds are told,
    And sorrow's tale still claims its meed of tears.
Britannia weeps Isandlwana's fray,
    And hangs her head in mingled grief and shame,
But proudly, smiling, lifts her trident high,
    To write " Rorke's Drift " upon the scroll of
    Fame,
Where " Cressy " " Poictiers," " Trafalgar " blaze
With other glorious names of by-gone days.

When drunk with triumph from that fearful fight,
    Whose memory haunts us like some hideous dream,
The Zulu host its swarthy myriads rolled
    On towards the passage of the border stream ;
What could resist that torrent's headlong rush,
    And turn its furious current whence it came,
Could save Natal with all its helpless souls,
    And re-assert the might of England's name ?

No mighty force was near to face the foe,
No arm seemed strong enough to strike the blow.

But He who sets the mighty ocean bounds,
    And bids each planet circle in its place,
Gives not the battle always to the strong,
    Nor yet the race to him of swiftest pace.
A puny host—about a hundred men—
    Performed the feat an army might have done;
Two nameless leaders swayed the gallant band,
    And ere the morn their golden spurs were won.
One hundred *soldiers* girded them for fight,
And eighty *heroes* saw the morning light.

Some straggling horsemen, plying whip and spur,
    Fugitives from Isandlwana's fray,   [tale,
Had reached Rorke's Drift, rehearsed their fearful
    Then urged their course where rest and safety lay.
Thus warned, the garrison their post prepare,
    To meet the foe that Rumour said was nigh;
With wagons, boxes, sacks of flour and grain,
    And aught to hand the place they fortify;

Slender defence, but, manned by Britons bold,
Stronger than strongest fort which cowards hold.

Scarce had these few their hurried rampart raised,
  When o'er that ridge long scanned by anxious
    eyes,
The Zulu host, in masses broad and deep,
  Approached in silence hoping to surprise.
Like some dark cloud portending dreadful storm,
  And from whose depths the lightnings soon will
    glance,
Sweeping in gloom across the darkened sky,
  So seemed, to those who watched, the foe's
    advance.
But they who stood behind that wall at bay,
Were like the wind to drive that cloud away.

A puff of fleecy smoke, a sharp report—
  The Zulu chief falls by a British hand;
And rifles, levelled with unerring aim,
  Make dreadful havoc in his chiefless band;
But on they rush, beneath that scathing fire,

Heedless of death, or wounds, or comrades
 slain ;
Like some huge billow rolling towards the strand,
 When tempests lash to rage the treacherous
 main.
Then, like that wave recoiling, back they fall,
Baffled and broken, from the guarded wall.

As some fierce beast, foiled by a slighted foe,
 With rage redoubled from the contest hies ;
Soon, with fresh force, the combat to renew,
 And strain each nerve to snatch the victor's
 prize ;
So the fierce foe his broken host withdraws,
 To seek a shelter from the leaden shower,
Thence, rested, reinforced, to charge once more,
 And crush resistance with resistless power.
Now gallant Britons ! quit yourselves like men,
And drive their savage legions back again !

Oh ! for the presence of that prophet-chief,
 Who stayed the fiery sun o'er Gibeon's height,

And stopped, above the Vale of Ajalon,
    The silvery chariot of the Queen of Night;
For twilight's shades descending wrap the scene,
    And shroud in favouring gloom the attacking foe;
Some, from the heights above, their volleys pour
    In murderous hail upon the fort below;
While others screened by Evening's shady pall
Essay once more to storm the guarded wall.

What words can paint that night's terrific fray,
    Illumined soon by War's own lurid light?
Can tell of desperate charge and countercharge
    Of Zulu prowess foiled by British might;
Of fierce attack repelled by stern defence,
    Of showers of bullets, clouds of hurtling spears,
The blazing pile revealing clustering foes,
    The Zulu shouts, the answering British cheers,
Which through the watches of that dreadful night
Announced the varying progress of the fight?

As dawn approached the horrid tumult ceased,
    And morning showed the foe in full retreat,

While hard-won Victory crowned the smoke-grimed
    brows
Of those who felt her welcome hour was sweet.
Thinned were their ranks by warfare's fatal shafts,
    Their bodies weary with protracted strife,
But knitted brows, clenched teeth, raised arms pro-
    claim
    Resistance still, resistance to the knife !
Then the hoarse cheer triumphant mounted high,
And e'en the wounded joined the joyous cry.

Oh, faithful few, Britannia's warrior sons,
    Proud Victors, worthy all of loftiest praise !
Would that some laurelled bard in deathless lines,
    Had shrined your deeds till Times' remotest days.
Perchance even he who sang " The Light Brigade "
    May once again resume his sounding lyre,
And to a listening world your glory tell
    In verses pregnant with celestial fire,
When these weak lines, unworthy of their theme,
Have found a resting place in Lethe's stream.

The Victoria Cross.

Not of gold with glitt'ring diamonds
    Is the ornament I sing,
But the soldier holds it dearer
    Than the jewels of a king.

'Tis a cross of simple pattern,
    Worthless in the huckster's eye;
But the soldier gives his life-blood oft,
    This *worthless* thing to buy.

No ancient, foreign motto
    Decks this cross, whose days are young,
But the trumpet words " For Valour,"
    In the grand old English tongue.

Peer and private wear it proudly,
    For the Queenly Heart who gave
Confesses all men equal
    In the Legion of the Brave.

Dusky Cross! so full of brightness
　　In the dauntless soldier's sight,
May you ever deck the bosoms
　　Of the champions of the right!

And where'er the might of England
　　Is seen in war array,
We shall find brave hearts resolving—
　　" I will win the cross to-day."

Private Brown's Christmas Eve.

The sentry walks on the rampart high,
　　The lights of the town gleam faint below;
And Heaven's bright lamps from the vault above,
　　Shed their silv'ry light o'er the virgin snow.

'Tis Christmas Eve; and the soldier hears,
　　As he paces slowly to-and-fro,
That grand old song which the angels sang
　　O'er the heights of Bethlehem long ago.

" Sweet Peace on Earth ; unto men good-will,"
    The heavenly numbers still proclaim ;
Though man make war on his fellow-man,
    God's message of love is still the same.

As the sweet sounds rise through the frosty air,
    From the " waits " below in the sleeping town,
A chord harmonious—silent long—
    Is struck in the heart of Private Brown.

His thoughts fly back to the happy past,
    And a fairy scene in his sight appears ;
Clear, and distinct, and full of life,
    Not blurred and dimmed by the mist of years.

He is back once more in the old loved home,
    He feels the grasp of a father's hand,
A mother's arms his neck entwine,
    And smiling sisters around him stand.

The season's sports attention claim,
    And he is " blindman " once again,
With outstretched arms and cautious steps
    Eagerly chasing the laughing train.

Then with ardour fired in the merry chase,
    And heedless grown of occasional knocks,
With a sudden rush he clasps to his breast
    The fairy form—of the sentry box.

The spell is broken, the clock strikes twelve :
    Five minutes more, and the welcome tread
Of the drowsy relief breaks on the ear ;
    And Brown soon sleeps on the guard-room bed.

The Soldier's Farewell. *

A Song.

Darling, ere the trumpet's warning
    Calls me sadly from thy side,
Ere I go at duty's summons,
    Kiss me once again, my bride !

* This song has been set to music by Herr Gecks. bandmaster,
R. W. Fusiliers.

Oh! the pain, the pain of parting,
  Tongue of mortal ne'er can tell,
Fiercest pangs of human anguish
  Centre in that word—Farewell.
Chorus:—Sweet wife, Farewell! those words now
    spoken,
  Roseate dreams of bliss dispel,
  Lives are sundered, hearts are broken,
  By that tearful word—Farewell.

Listen, darling, ere we're severed,
  Listen to a soldier's vow;
Fondly, madly have I loved thee,
  But I love thee dearer now
In this agony of parting,
  When each heart-beat seems a knell,
O'er the grave of hopes and pleasures,
  Buried 'neath that word—Farewell.
Chorus:—Sweet wife, Farewell! those words now
    spoken,
  Roseate dreams of bliss dispel,
  Lives are sundered, hearts are broken,
  By that tearful word—Farewell.

By those tears that shine so brightly,
In thine eyes of azure hue,
Like the pearly drops of morning,
Glitt'ring on the violets blue.
By the lily in thy cheek, love,
Where the rose was wont to dwell;
I am thine and thine for ever,
Though I now must say—Farewell!

Chorus:—Sweet wife, Farewell! those words now
spoken,
Roseate dreams of bliss dispel,
Lives are sundered, hearts are broken,
By that tearful word—Farewell.

———

British Soldiers.

A VISION.

I saw them—led by Marlbro'
  'Gainst the vet'ran troops of France,
And my heart beat high with patriot pride
  To see their brave advance;
For they swept the field before them
  With their levelled English steel,
And they fought, and bled, and conquered,
  And died for England's weal.

I saw them—on that Belgian plain.
  Beneath th' Iron Duke's eye,
Standing steadfast, grim, and silent,
  Resolved to do or die.
Steel-clad cuirassier and lancer
  Broke against that stubborn host,
As the waves of angry ocean
  Break on the British coast.

I saw them—ford the Alma
　　Lashed to foam by leaden hail,
I marked that wild Death's Valley ride,
　　When not a cheek turned pale.
Of the twice three hundred horsemen
　　Who galloped side by side,
Charging home the wide world's wonder,
　　And their native country's pride.

I saw them—in an Empire,
　　Which their arms had bravely won,
They were in a 'leaguered city,
　　Beneath a burning sun ;
Under the sainted Havelock,
　　A gallant band they stood,
And England's prisoned daughters
　　Were ransomed with their blood.

I saw them—and methought this scene
　　The grandest sight of all,
It beat the wild Death's Valley ride,
　　And Lucknow's guarded wall ;

All honour to the noble dead,
    All honour to the brave,
Who with the fated ' Birkenhead '
    Went down beneath the wave!

I saw them—standing calmly,
    Knowing well that Death was nigh,
" Save the women and the children,
    As for us oh we can die."
Farewell ye red-coat heroes!
    Farewell devoted band!
I would have left the proudest place,
    On that sinking deck to stand.

I saw them—home in England,
    Upon their native shore.
Honoured and admired? no, hated,
    And despised because they wore
That garb in which they triumphed,
    Round which our history clings,
That garb which should be honoured
    As the robes of England's kings.

The Unofficial Inspection.*

In that lofty hill station, Panchbattie by name,
An adventure occurred lately—unknown to fame ;
But now 'tis enshrined in the verse of a poet,
So renowned as the present the world will soon
       know it :

    Major-General George Fitzclay
    Had notified in the usual way,
    That he shortly expected a visit to pay,
    To inspect and report in the regular way
    On the discipline, drill, and books galore,
    Kits and rifles and things in store ;
    And—I forget—but something more,
    Of that distinguished Infantry corps
    (Lately stationed at Dumpipore

---

* This poem is founded upon a well-known incident, which
happened at Chakrata, when the Royal Welsh were stationed
at " that lofty hill-station."

But now at Panchbattie a year or more)
Which a very euphonious title bore,
And on its colours and badges wore
A Griffin, and Sphinx, and something more.

When this notification was published and read
   To this Infantry corps we have mentioned before,
Some got most decidedly light in the head,
   And some in their nervousness actually *swore ;*
For though General's Inspection comes every year,
It always makes some people feel rather queer.

   The officers started with right good-will
   To cram as much as they could of drill,
   And calmly swallowed the bitter pill,
   Although it made some of them rather ill.

Harry Fitz Poole, the swell of the mess,
Had scarcely even time to dress ;
And Tommy Chaffer, the soul of fun,
Never gave vent to joke or pun,

But button-holed comrades by night and day,
And conundrums asked in an anxious way,
Such as—" What is a private's daily pay ? "
" Can you tell me the price of shirts and socks,"
" Or the cubic contents of a blacking box ? "
" What's a man stopped when fined for drunk ?"
In short they were all in a terrible funk,
Excepting of course the intelligent cards
Who know Regulations and Drill by yards.

The battalion was drilled till it seemed quite
  perfection
In the usual routine of a General's Inspection.
      They marched-up and down,
        At " shoulder " and " trail,"
      As straight as a plank,
        And as right as the mail.
      Their " Manual " was perfect,
        Their " Firing " likewise,
      And they licked all creation
        At Bayonet Ex'rcise.

Major-General George Fitzclay
Is expected now in a week and a day :
A week—six days—five days—now four—oh !
Three days—two days—he comes to-morrow.
The Regiment paraded at four P. M.,
Under Sergeant-Major Phlegm,
To receive the last tips required for them.
And on calling the roll of number three
Private Jones was absent. Where could he be ?
It was shrewdly suspected on the spree.
For Private Jones was a jovial soul
And dearly loved the flowing bowl ;
He'd spend his money, and sell his clothes,
To muddle his brains, and colour his nose,
And now 'twas concluded he'd " spouted " his kit
And was somewhere busily drinking it.

      *   *   *   *

The Parade went on in the usual way,   [stay !
" Left wheel into line ! " " Quick march"—now
Who is that officer over the way,
Touching his cap as the bandsmen play
And the Line " presents " in the usual way ?

Why 'tis Major-General George Fitzclay,
Privately noting the corps' display,
In quite an unofficial way.

He must have arrived by the *kutcha* road
Over the hills from his late abode.

     *   *   *   *

Not a man in the ranks that afternoon,
But saw the General, plain as the moon,
When she rides serene through a cloudless sky,
And they all resolved " to do or die."

Never, I ween, was such smartness seen
In any corps that serves the Queen,
As in that old corps which the Griffin wore,
The Sphinx, White Horse, and something more,
As they " shoulder'd," and " ported," and
    " charged " before
      Major-General George Fitzclay,
      In a perfectly unofficial way.

     *   *   *   *

Five o'clock struck on the guard-room gong,
But none of the men thought the hour too long,
For each one felt, as he drilled that day,

He was under the eye of General Fitzclay,
Although in an unofficial way;
And now 'twas over each man could tell
That the Regiment had never drilled half so well.

     *   *   *   *

The Sergeant-Major stalked away
To ask the permission of General Fitzclay
To dismiss the men—not as though they were tired,
But simply because—their hour had expired.
As the Sergeant-Major approached ; Fitzclay,
With a courtesy Generals always display,
Advanced to meet the man half-way ;
    When, strange to say,
    General Fitzclay
    Fell straightway,
    Into the gutter, and there he lay.
Fell into the gutter that bounded the square
And lay as if quite contented there.
Now the Sergeant-Major felt very queer,
And his feelings increased when he came quite near,
And saw, that the bundle of flesh and bones,
Which all had mistaken for General Fitzclay,

Inspecting the drill in a casual way,
Was the body that answered to " Evan Jones,"
" Thirteen hundred and seventy-three,"
Right hand man of his company,
The man who'd absented himself d'ye see,
And 'twas shrewdly suspected was on the spree.
Dressed in an old theatrical suit,
The General quite, from cap to boot.

A couple of files with a corporal bore
The " General " safe to the Guard-room floor,
Where he slept all night with many a snore ;
And his " chums " in the barrack-room laughed
    and swore
That they never had heard of the like before.

The " *pukhah* " General came next day,
The *real* General George Fitzclay,
And inspected the corps in the usual way.

The old corps did as they always do,
And the General said—and he spoke quite true
They were ready to do, as they'd always done,

March and fight anywhere under the sun.
He dined at Mess in the good old way,
  And heartily laughed when the Colonel told,
Of his pseudo-self of the previous day,
  And how the men were so dreadfully sold.

Next day he called up Evan Jones,
" Thirteen hundred and seventy-three,"
Right hand man of his company,
The man who'd been absent and on the spree ;
And, after declaring he'd set him free ;
He strongly advised him to join " T. T."
And never more in earnest or fun,
To do again as he'd lately done—
Personify General George Fitzclay,
And inspect troops in that unofficial way.

———

The Darwinian Theory.

Some curious theories are now propounded,
At which plain people well may be astounded ;
Of most of them I have my own opinion,
But still I doubtful feel of the Darwinian ;
And this short story which I now relate
May interest thinkers in a doubtful state.
A soldier, travelling lately, learnt the style
(To use a vulgar phrase I hate the while)
Of keeping open wide his " weather eye,"
And noting carefully what passed him by.
While following out this self-improving plan,
Which I would recommend to every man,
One thing upon his mind was much impressed,
People's aversion to the way he dressed.
'Twas not so much his coat's *cut* as its *colour*
Which seemed to rouse all virtuous people's choler.
Into whate'er society he came,
Clergy or Laity, 'twas all the same.

He quickly noticed all turn up their noses
In that peculiar way which hate discloses.
Happening one day to visit at a farm,
With pain the soldier saw the wild alarm
And anger which his presence caused among
The bulls and turkey-cocks, both old and young ;
Cause of offence to bull and turkey-cock
Being nothing but the colour of his frock.
Now he being of a philosophic mind,
To reasoning by analogy inclined,
Was doubtful putting this and that together
The good folks', bulls', and turkeys' choler whether
It did not show for scarlo-phobist fools
A clear descent from turkey-cocks or bulls.
To this opinion he so much inclined,
No argument had power to change his mind.
He'd still maintain the truth of his conclusion
By powerful arguments in great profusion,
By weak-kneed logic of a novel plan,
And long extracts from the " Descent of Man."

———

"Sweet are the Uses of Adversity."

Apollo's car had vanished—
    For that's the poet's way
Of announcing to his readers
    That it was the close of day.

Yes, the sun had set in India,
    Where, as all the world doth know,
India's scorched Feringhee guardians
    Are glad to see him go.

'Twas seven P. M., bewitching hour!
    For me post-prandial time,
Aye to Nicotina sacred,
    And sometimes, as now, to rhyme.

Buried in the depths cavernous
    Of my favourite easy-chair,
Hid by aromatic vapours,
    I reclined, absolved from care.

Near me Punch, *Pœtæ canis*,
　　Lay intent upon a bone,
Which a wicked-looking pariah
　　Seemed to wish that he might own.

I, of both alike oblivious,
　　Dozed in the waning light,
When my ears were rudely startled
　　By the sounds of canine fight.

Looking up I saw poor Punchie
　　'Neath that wicked pariah prone,
That bad dog's ulterior motive
　　Being to possess the bone.

All my soul with ardour burning,
　　Quick to Punch's aid I ran,
And in quest of useful missile,
　　Stretched out my dexter hand.

Stick and stone were at a discount,
　　But, convenient to my chair,
Lay a clothes-brush, which some Hindoo
　　Of my household had left there.

Gladly seizing this projectile,
  With a giant's force I threw
It at that pariah's cranium
  With an aim both swift and true.

And that pariah, when the clothes-brush
  Hit him straight between the eyes,
As was quite to be expected,
  Raised a howl of wild surprize.

Thus to smite the rash intruder
  Filled my soul with wondrous glee,
But his subsequent proceedings
  Raised astonishment in me.

For he gave one swift appraising look
  At the missile I had sent,
Then seized it 'twixt his thieving fangs
  And homewards bounding went.

With a mortifying feeling,
  And no longer filled with glee,
In my chair I sought for comfort
  From my evening cup of tea.

Soon my mind, beneath its influence,
　　Rallied, and resumed its tone,
While " Punch " in quiet possession
　　Lay munching at his bone ;

And methought this pariah's conduct
　　Gave to man a lesson plain,
To make gladness spring from sorrow,
　　And take profit out of pain.

Thus, if Brown, by anger prompted,
　　Threw at Jones's head a brick,
Jones, instead of mauling Brown
　　With retaliatory stick,

Were to calmly lift that brick,
　　And never glance at Brown at all,
But coolly take it homewards
　　To repair his garden-wall ;

Brown the vicious would go homewards
　　Feeling altogether " done,"
While the virtuous Jones would chuckle
　　O'er his chop to think he'd won.

The words which form the title
  Of this string of silly rhyme,
Are to most folks quite familiar
  In this literary time.

So I sha'n't insult my readers,
  Who I trust in crowds abound,
By presuming to inform them
  Where those words are to be found.

They are words of truth and comfort,
  Which I thought I knew aright,
Till that pariah's wise proceeding
  Showed them in another light.

Lines written on the Death, by drowning, of Private Alfred Udall, R. W. Fusiliers.

Though Nature to-day wear her sunniest smile,
  Dull to me seems the landscape, and gloomy the
  skies,
For he whom my soul loved with more than Earth's
  love,
  In the clammy embrace of the Terror King lies.

And Nature's bright smile seems but ill to accord
  With the sorrowful gloom that o'ershadows my
  brow,
And Earth's "thousand voices," that erst seemed
  so sweet,
  Sound harsh, or discordant, or sad to me now.

Beneath his red coat beat as knightly a heart,
  As ever pulsated 'neath corslet of steel,
And he owned, what is rare in this Mammonite age,
  A hand that would help, and a heart that could
  feel.

I am told he had faults—there are spots on the sun
    And 'tis not for friendship those faults to proclaim,
But I *knew* him so gentle, so noble, and true,
    That my ears must be deaf to attacks on his
        fame.

This garland of wild flowers I lay on his tomb,
    Rude rhymes from a heart that in life loved him
        well,
The Muse's weak effort in numbers to show
    Those pangs of the soul which no language can
        tell.

The Crusader.

In the beautiful Adela's lovely bower,
    A sorrowful scene takes place to-day ;
For young Maurice, her knight, in his armour
        bright,
    Comes to say Farewell ! and bid her pray
That the Virgin may save and keep him well
In the distant land of the Infidel.

As she fastens her glove in her lover's crest,
  Deep are the sighs of that lady fair ;
And a tear unbid to the knight's eye starts,
  As he toys with a tress of her golden hair ;
But he checks his grief, though his heart is
    pained,
As unworthy the knighthood so lately gained.

His page and squire in the courtyard wait,
  With his steeds arrayed in warlike gear ;
So he presses one kiss to his lady's lips,
  And whispers ' Courage ' in her ear ;
Then, with clanking step, to the courtyard strides,
Where the squire th'impatient charger chides.

And mounting, away o'er the drawbridge he
    rides,
  Under the grim portcullis, whose teeth,
Ever ready to drop at the sight of a foe,
  Look threateningly down on the portal beneath,
He goes in his Love and young life's spring,
To join the array of the Lion-heart King.

And Adela weeps in her lonely bower,
   And night and morn to Heaven doth kneel,
That Sir Maurice be saved from all danger near,
   From wizard's spell and Paynim's steel,
From perils by land, or by ocean wave,
She prayeth Our Lady her knight to save.

But her prayers were vain, for the knight was
   slain
   In that Holy Land he loved so well.
The foremost Lance in the Christian host
   In Arsoof's fight he nobly fell ;
Pressing in death to his gallant breast
The glove she had bound 'neath his helmet's crest.

When tidings come to Old England's shores,
   Of the deeds and fame of her warlike King,
The Nation's heart beats high with joy,
   And loud through the land his praises ring ;
But one heart, full of a selfish grief,
In a nation's joy finds no relief.

Fair Adela, long in the cloistered shades,
  Mourned the loss of her brave young knight,
And the world seemed sad and full of gloom,
  That erst had looked so fair and bright,
Till by precept taught, and example fair,
She humbly learned her cross to bear.

The Two Valentines.

In the days of the golden past love,
  When our hearts were still in their spring,
When the months seemed weeks and the weeks
        seemed days,
  As Time flew past on unheeded wing.

I sent you a missive then, my love,
  A beautiful marvel of paper design,
With Cupids, and hearts transfixed by darts,
  In short an elegant Valentine.

Though those days are past and gone, my love,
　And our hearts beat calmer than of yore,
Still the light of love from thine angel-eyes
　Shines steadily now as it did before.

And our passion, though now never talked of, love,
　I know is still leal and true,
As ever it was in that golden past,
　Which is sacred to Love and you.

So I send you a token again, love,
　On this St. Valentine's day,
A token to tell, what you know well,
　That my love, though old, has not passed away.

A plain little card with a border, love,
　In the centre a true-lover's knot,
And the words in gold, on an azure field,
　" I love thee, dearest ! forget me not."

Retrospection.

Kindly thoughts are o'er me stealing,
    As I think on Youth's bright day ;
In my ears the school-bell pealing,
    Sounds a chorus to my lay.

And oh! that love of childhood,
    With a fairy form so slight,
Seems nearer, dearer, clearer in
    My mem'ry's eye to-night.

Passion's fire hath scourged my bosom,
    And run riot through my heart,
Yet it ne'er effaced that mem'ry,
    Of my life the purest part.

No, the pure flame still burns brightly,
    Laugh cynic as you may ;
Its clear light, o'er my wayward heart,
    Still sends a cheering ray.

Which, like the friendly home-light
  To the storm-tossed sailor's gaze,
Speaks to me of a refuge,
  And a hope for better days.

Cousin Nellie.

Charming, fair-haired, cousin Nellie!
  You are in my thoughts to-night,
And your presence felt so near me,
  Thrills me with a sweet delight.

Oh! how well we loved each other,
  In that glorious summer weather,
Laughing, sporting, flirting, loving
  Morning, noon, and eve together.

When decoyed by fairy legends,
  Through the fields your way you took,
There to see your future lover
  Mirrored in the shining brook.

4

I, in ambush, watched thee, Nellie,
   Tremblingly approach the place,
Smiled to see your disappointment,
   Seeing but your own sweet face.

Fairer picture ne'er was mirrored,
   In that clear brook's shady stream,
Fairer form than thine, dear Nellie!
   Ne'er was rhyming soldier's theme.

Oh! how bravely when we parted
   Tossed on high that pretty head,
But one pearly tear-drop falling
   Rested on my coat of red.

By that tear-drop's pearly lustre!
   By my faith and hope for bliss!
Ne'er shall other lips than thine, love,
   Take again thy parting kiss.

To Lizzie.

Though your years, my little Venus,
   Don't exceed the sum of four,
And your curly pate scarce reaches
   To the handle of my door ;

Though your best articulation
   Sounds sometimes rather odd,
And your usual affirmation
   Is an arbitrary nod ;

Yet your honest broken prattle
   Sounds far sweeter in my ears,
Than the vapid conversation
   Vented oft by older " dears."

You frankly say you love me, dear,
   Then most surely am I blest,
Even though I hear you sometimes say
   That you love your kitten best.

Not a thought of rings or necklets
   E'er into your mind intrudes,
And a lollipop's sufficient
   To appease your surliest moods.

For a beau with slender income
   You're the belle young sweetheart mine,
So till Mammon swells my coffers
   I will worship at thy shrine.

———

To the New Year (1875).

Centuries have gone since, upon Bethlehem's plains,
   Angels from Heaven proclaimed Messiah's birth.
Centuries may still elapse before His name
   Is known and praised by every tongue on earth,
But oh ! may this, and each New Year, increase
The present prospects of the Reign of Peace.

Full of bright hope we hail thee then—New Year,
   And may'st thou realize our fairest dreams ;
Sorrow and care no doubt thy days will bring,
   But think not now of such unpleasant themes ;
We'll know thy history who thy course survive,
Meanwhile with smiles we greet thee—Seventy-
   five.

Masonic Song.

Air :—" SCATTER SEEDS OF KINDNESS."

*Dedicated to the Brethren of St. David's Lodge,
R. W. Fusiliers.*

Brethren of the " square and compass "
   Seated now in social throng !
Speeding on the golden moments
   With the joyous toast and song,

Let us not forget Life's troubles
 Mid the pleasures of to-day,
But stretch a hand to brethren
 Who may lag upon the way.

Chorus :—And hand in hand together,
 In calm or stormy weather,
 We'll journey o'er Life's pathway
 To the Lodge beyond the sky.

In the busy world around us
 There are many ups and downs,
And our brightest hopes are blighted oft
 By Fortune's cruel frowns ;
But fair or foul may craftsmen still,
 Howe'er they fall or stand,
Never lack the kindly pressure,
 Of a loyal brother's hand.

Chorus :—And hand in hand together,
 In calm or stormy weather,
 We'll journey o'er Life's pathway
 To the Lodge beyond the sky.

Let us order well our conduct,
  By the plummet's rigid rule,
Heedless of the scorner's scoffing,
  Or the laughter of the fool.
Let us ponder well the lessons,
  That our tools of labour teach ;
And show the world around us
  That we practise what we preach.

Chorus :—And hand in hand together,
    In calm or stormy weather,
    We'll journey o'er Life's pathway
    To the Lodge beyond the sky.

Autumn.

The changing hue of the trees,
  The falling leaves in the lane,
And the russet tints of the heathy down,
Seem to say with no uncertain sound
  " The year is on the wane."

I love ripe autumn well
    With his gay fruit-laden train,
But his falling leaves, and fading flowers,
Awake sad thoughts in our gayest hours—
    The year is on the wane.

'Tis only another year
    With its blended joy and pain,
Gliding away to the wondrous Past,
So slowly to some, to others so fast,
    But surely on the wane.

And of hosts of human lives
    May be sung the same refrain,
For millions, alas! in this world of ours,
Like the dying year and its fading flowers,
    Are surely on the wane.

Summer.

To Nellie.

Oh who could think of being sad in June,
  That leafiest, loveliest month of all the year ;
When Nature's choristers all sing in tune
  Their sweetest songs to every listening ear ?
When even our dull sky is sometimes seen
  With that of sunnier climes to vie in hue,
And fleecy clouds piled stately and serene
  Appear like mountains on the ethereal blue.

Such were my thoughts, as on the " gowan lea,"
  Beneath a spreading branch I idly lay ;
From every care or thought of trouble free,
  Seeing the Future through the bright To-day ;
Lulled by the sound of drowsy insects' wings,
  Pleased with the grateful smell of sweetest
    flowers,
I laughed to scorn the petty pomps of kings,
  And dreamt of Love, and walked his golden
    bowers.

Though to my eyes Dame Nature had displayed
   As fair a scene as man could e'er survey,
Hid were the various beauties of the glade
   To me, for oh! my thoughts were far away—
With thee, my darling, in that distant dell,
   Which first beheld our mutual plighted love,
When one soft sigh, and one sweet kiss, dear Nell,
   Settled the compact, and the stars above

Looked calmly down upon the scene so fair,
   Heaven's own bright witnesses of lovers' vows.
Oh, happy hour! oh, "bliss beyond compare"!
   Which Jove to mankind once in life allows—
That first fond kiss and mutual caressing
   Of Youth and Maiden in their young Love's
     bloom,
Each blessed and each bestowing sweetest blessing
   The happiest hour to man this side the tomb.

Acrostics.

LOTTIE.

" Be *good*, sweet mind, let those who will be *clever*."

Kingsley.

Let those be *clever*, dear, who would be so,
Only remember *talent* ne'er wins *love ;*
Try to be *good* as through this world you go,
Trusting for helps to One who sits above ;
In times of darkness look for light to Him,
Enthroned between the glorious cherubim.

M. E. MORRISON.

(Written in an Album.)

My Album this, where friends may write their names,
Enlarge upon the topics of the day,
Make neat quotations from their favourite books,
Or on pet subjects have their little " say ";
Record in various styles their loves or woes,
(Reaping applause or laughter for their pains)

In halting verse, or mayhap jumbled prose,
　Showing to all their wealth, or want, of brains.
One thing is certain, those who use my page
Need never fear the envious critic's rage.

A Roundel.

(*After* ALGERNON SWINBURNE.)

Dear wife, thou ministering angel, who
　Mak'st smooth for me the stony path of life,
Dark were my day if thou wert lost to view,
　　　Dear wife !
When weary with the burden of my life,
　I think of thee, so tender, leal, and true,
I bless thee, Heaven ! who gave me such a wife.

Thou art, my darling, of God's chosen few
　Who shed sweet peace around them in the strife,
And so I dedicate this verse to you,
　　　Dear wife !